Malorie Blackman

My Friend's a Gris-Kwok

With illustrations by

Andy Rowland

Barrington Stoke

First published in 2013 in Great Britain by
Barrington Stoke Ltd
18 Walker Street, Edinburgh, EH3 7LP

www.barringtonstoke.co.uk

This story was first published in a different form as
My Friend's a Gris-Quok (Scholastic, 1994)

Text © 2013 Oneta Malorie Blackman
Illustrations © Andy Rowland

ISBN: 978-1-78112-244-0

Printed in China by Leo

This book has dyslexia friendly features

For Neil and Lizzy,
with love as always

www.malorieblackman.co.uk

Contents

1 How it Began   1

2 The First Change   16

3 Splinters Like Trees   32

4 Scaredy Cat   62

5 No Backwards, No Forwards, No Sideways   75

Chapter 1
How it Began

My best friend Alex is a Gris-Kwok!

I know what you're thinking. What's a Gris-Kwok?

Well, I didn't know either. But then I found out Alex's secret. And this is how it happened ...

Early one Saturday morning, I popped over to Alex's house. Just as I rang his doorbell, a drop of rain splashed on my cheek. I looked up at the grey sky, and then I saw someone at the bedroom window.

It was Alex's awful little sister, Polly!

Alex opened the front door. "Hi, Mike!" he said with a grin. "Come in. Mum's out so we've got the house to ourselves for a while."

"I thought Polly's bedroom was at the back of the house?" I said.

"It is," Alex said. "Why?"

"Well, I saw her in the front bedroom," I said. "She's making funny faces at me out the window." I pointed up at her. "Very funny faces."

"**What?**" Alex stepped outside to see what was going on.

I started to make faces back at Polly. I pulled my lips one way and my cheeks the other and screwed up my eyes.

"Mike, you're as bad as Polly. Come on." Alex grabbed my arm and dragged me into the house. He kicked the door shut behind us and ran upstairs.

I wondered what all the fuss was about as I ran after him. I soon found out. Alex went straight to his mum and dad's bedroom. He turned the door handle, but the door didn't open.

"She's ... she's locked the door!" Alex was so angry. He bent to peer through the keyhole, and then he stood up almost at once.

"Polly! Open this door right this **second**!" he yelled.

Behind the door, I could hear Polly laughing her head off. Alex hammered on the door.

"Polly, I'm warning you. If you don't come out, I'll tell Mum and Dad and then you'll be in major trouble!" Alex bent to peep through the keyhole again.

"What's she doing?" I asked.

"Spraying Mum's posh perfume all over herself," Alex shouted.

I bit my lip to stop myself from laughing out loud.

"I should never have taken my eyes off her," Alex said. "Not for a moment. Mum warned me not to leave her by herself."

"It's not your fault," I began. "You'll just have to ..."

But Alex wasn't listening. "**Polly!**" he shouted. "**Polly, don't you dare!**"

"What's the matter? What's she doing now?" I asked.

"Rats! She's just turned herself into a bird and she's ... Oops!" Alex slapped his hand over his mouth as he turned to look at me. "Rats! My mouth is bigger than the number 19 bus!"

I stared at him.

"What did you say?" I asked. "Polly's turned herself into a **what**?"

"A ... a bird," Alex said. "A robin, I think. And she's flying around the room."

Chapter 2
The First Change

I put my fingers into my ears and wiggled them about.

"My ears aren't working," I said. "It sounded like you just said Polly had turned into a bird!"

"She has. She's a robin," Alex said.
His eye was pressed to the keyhole
again.

"Alex, I think that keyhole is doing
something to your eyes – or your brain,"
I said.

Alex stood up and turned to me.

"Mike, can you keep a secret?" he asked.

"Of course I can," I said. "What is it?"

"I'm going to tell you something," he said. "But you must promise that you'll **never** tell anyone else. Not even your mum and dad. And you must promise not to tell my mum and dad that I told you."

"I promise," I said right away.

"All right then," he said. "I think it'll be easier if I just show you. Hold on to my jumper."

"Why do I have to ...?"

"Never mind that now," Alex said. "We don't have much time. We've got to get in there before it's too late. Polly's going to hurt herself. She doesn't know what she's doing."

"But we can't get through a locked door," I said.

"Grab hold of my jumper," Alex ordered.

I did as he said.

"Ready?" he asked.

"Ready for what?"

"I'll explain later," he said. "Here we go!"

All of a sudden I felt very strange
indeed. I felt squeezed and squashed
and bunched up and hunched up. My
whole body tickled and prickled, my back
most of all. I looked down, then stared.

Where were my feet? Where were
my shoes? My legs had gone and the
carpet seemed a long, long way down.
It was like being in a plane and looking
down at the ground far below.

And where was Alex?

I looked around. I couldn't see Alex anywhere, but there was a fly right in front of me. A horrible, hairy, **huge** fly! A whooshing sound filled the air. I was amazed when I realised it was the sound of the fly's wings beating.

And the fly was heading for me!

"Zzzz!" I squeaked as I tried to get out of its way.

I didn't move fast enough. **Slap!** The fly hit me.

I felt myself falling, falling, falling to the ground. Bump! I looked down. My legs were back. So were my feet – and my shoes! I looked around, confused. Where was the fly?

And more importantly, where was Alex?

Without warning, Alex appeared. It was so sudden, I blinked several times to make sure my eyes were working.

One moment Alex wasn't there, the next moment he was.

"Why did you smack into me?" Alex asked. He had his arms folded.

I scrambled to get up. "What do you mean?" I asked. "There was a huge fly coming straight for me and it banged into me ..."

Alex was so annoyed that his eyebrows almost joined up. "That was me, idiot," he said. "I was the fly!"

Chapter 3
Splinters Like Trees

I must have heard Alex wrong.

"Pardon?" I said.

"That was me," Alex said again. "I turned into a fly. You turned into one too, because you were touching me when I changed."

"I turned into a fly?" I shook my head. "Oh, come off it, Alex!"

"It's true, I promise," Alex said. "You turned into a fly. You were flying and everything. But I didn't have a chance to explain what I'd done before you came flying at me. And then you touched me again and you changed back."

"Hang on a minute," I said. "I didn't fly at **you**. **You** bumped into **me**."

"Look, Mike, can we talk about which
of us bumped into the other one later?"
Alex said. "Right now we have to catch
Polly before she gets us all into big
trouble. So hold onto my jumper while
you change, then let go. When you've
turned into a fly, don't touch me again
until we've both flown through the
keyhole. OK?"

I was too puzzled to argue, so I did as Alex said and took hold of his jumper.

He started to change and so did I. The feeling of being squeezed and squashed and bunched up and hunched up came back, even stronger than before.

I looked down at my body. My arms
and legs had turned into thin stalks
covered in black hairs. My hands and
feet had vanished and I had things like
claws instead. But the strangest thing of
all was the tickling, prickling feeling in
my back.

At first it felt like something scratching me on both sides of my back. Then it felt as if my shoulder blades were stretching and growing and as if my skin was being pulled and pinched. It didn't hurt. But there was something very odd going on behind me.

Then I saw what it was.

Wings! I had wings! Yippee! They were wide and thin and very strong. I moved them together, then apart. I was flying. Wow!

"OK, Mike." Alex's voice was high and squeaky. "We're going to fly through the keyhole now," he said. "Stay close to me – but not too close – and be careful."

Alex flew towards the keyhole. I followed him. Whoosh! Whooosh! My wings beat through the air.

"Mike! Don't get too close to me!"
Alex called out.

I was so busy smiling at my wings
that I had forgotten to look where I was
going!

"Careful, Mike!" Alex warned me. "If you touch me when we're flying through the keyhole, you'll turn into a boy again, right in the middle of the door."

Ugh! That wasn't a very nice thought at all.

Alex flew right through the middle of the keyhole. I waited a second, then followed him. I looked around in surprise. All around me were huge, pale trees with no leaves on them. Then I saw that they weren't trees at all.

They were **splinters**. I was so tiny that the splinters looked like the tallest trees in our local park!

"What's that hazy stuff in the air?" I asked Alex.

"I'm not sure," he said. "I think it's dust. Our wings must be stirring up the dust in the keyhole."

I would never have guessed that there could be so much dust in one keyhole! It was all around me now. My nose began to tingle, then to tickle, then to itch.

"Ahhhh ... Ahhhh ... Alex ... I'm going ... to ..."

"Don't sneeze, Mike," Alex said. "Please! Hang on, or you'll crash into those splinter-tree things."

"I ... can't ... help ... it!" I gasped. "The dust t-t-tickles m-my nose ... aaa-aaa-aaa-aaa ..."

Just then we reached the other side
of the keyhole. Everything was brighter
and lighter. Alex flew back near me.

"Hang on, Mike, I'll change you back,"
he called out.

"Aaa-aaa-aaa-aaa-choo!" I sneezed.

The power of the sneeze sent me
flying backwards and I smacked hard
into Alex.

Blomp! We both landed on the ground with a thump. I sneezed again, "Aaa-aaa-aaa-aaa-choo!" And again. "Aaa-aaa-aaa-aaa-choo!" I got up and rubbed my itchy nose with one hand and my sore bum with the other.

"Mike, are you all right?" Alex asked.

I nodded.

"Good," he said. "Now we need to find my pesky sister. Polly ... Polly, where are you?" Alex walked further into the room. "You just wait till I get my hands on you!"

I looked around. There was no one in the room apart from me and Alex.

"Where is she then?" I asked.

Alex shook his head. "She's changed into something else. She's only just learned how to change, so now she does it whenever she can. She's a real pain!"

"I still don't understand what's going on," I moaned.

The key to the room was on a chair next to the door, so I picked it up and unlocked the door. At least that was one problem solved! Alex looked behind the dressing-table.

"How come you and your sister can change into something else any time you want to?" I asked, as Alex peeped behind the wardrobe. "Can you turn into chairs and planes and chewing-gum and things like that?"

"Polly and I are Gris-Kwoks," Alex said. "Well, we're half Gris-Kwok. You see, Mum's a Gris-Kwok, but Dad is just a normal human." Alex lifted up the duvet and peered under his mum and dad's bed. "We can't change into furniture or stuff like that," he told me. "We can only change into animals, birds, insects or fish, and we can only do it three times a day. Mum can change as often as she likes, because she's not half human like me and Polly."

"You look normal," I said.

"Yeah, I know," Alex said. He looked glum. "It's sad, isn't it?"

"Mind you, your mum looks normal too," I pointed out.

"Yeah, I know," Alex said. He looked even glummer. "It's a shame, really."

"A Gris-Kwok, though!" I said. "I've never heard of one of those before. Wow, you are lucky. I wish I could turn into something else whenever I wanted to."

"It was more fun before we all had to start chasing Polly around the house," Alex said. He sniffed sadly.

"You don't think she's done what we did and flown through the keyhole?" I asked.

I opened the door to see if Polly was out on the landing somewhere.

"No, Mike! Don't open the door ..."

Too late! A small, brown mouse appeared from nowhere and ran straight for my feet. It stood in front of me and squeaked up at me.

Then I really made a fool of myself.

"Arrggghhh! A mouse!" I jumped up onto a chair.

"Shut the door," Alex yelled.

He dived across the bed and ran to the door to slam it shut. But he was too late. The mouse ran out onto the landing and down the stairs.

"Rats! Rats! Rats!" Alex said. "We've lost her."

"Was that Polly?" I asked. I was still shuddering from seeing the mouse at my feet. I hate mice.

"Who else?" said Alex. "Come on, Mike. I've got a plan. I know how we can catch Polly for sure."

Chapter 4
Scaredy Cat

"Hold on to my jumper again," Alex said.

I grabbed hold. "So what are we going to be this time?" I asked. I was looking forward to it!

Alex didn't say a word, but I felt my body change again. I was shrinking, shrinking, shrinking. I fell on my hands and knees on the carpet. Then, as I watched, my hands began to change.

Thick, brown hair started to sprout out of my skin. My ears began to grow longer. Whiskers popped out from under my nose and the bottom of my back began to tingle. **Whish!** I had a tail!

"I'm a cat!" I said.

I looked down at my paws. They were covered with sleek brown fur. Just then I felt like I wanted to lick them. It was an odd feeling!

"Come on, Mike. My sister's getting away," Alex said.

We dashed down the stairs. When I was half way down, I stopped. I bent my legs, then jumped up onto the hand-rail. Easy! I looked down at the hall carpet. Then I jumped down, all the way into the hall. Double easy!

"Stop showing off, Mike," Alex said. "We've got to find Polly. You take the living room and I'll search the kitchen."

I ran into the living room and stopped just inside the door. I sniffed the air with my cat nose, then sniffed again.

"Alex, she's in here," I called out. "There's a strong smell of mouse in here."

Alex ran in. "Are you sure?"

"Positive." I nodded my head. "She's in here somewhere."

"Right! You stay by the door and I'll track her down," Alex said.

He ran behind the sofa to search for his sister. I marched up and down in front of the door.

"Squeak!" I looked around and saw Polly running towards me.

"Oh no you don't, Polly," I called out. "No way are you going to get past me again."

Now that I was a cat, I wasn't afraid of a little mouse!

I would have got her, if she hadn't played a dirty, mean trick.

I was just about to jump on Polly the mouse, when Polly the mouse vanished!

In her place was Polly the elephant!

Every last bit of fur on my body stood up on end. My tail fluffed out as I made up my mind that a cat was no match for an elephant. I was just about to make a dash for it when Alex skidded out from behind the sofa and banged right into me.

And **boof!** Just like that, we were boys again, with a great big elephant in front of us.

Chapter 5

No Backwards, No Forwards, No Sideways

"Polly, change back right this second!" Alex ordered.

Polly lifted her trunk and made a noise like a trumpet.

"Shhh!" Alex begged. "Or someone will hear you."

Polly lifted her trunk again and made an even louder noise than before!

"What's she's saying?" I whispered.

Alex shook his head. "I haven't
a clue," he said. "I've never been an
elephant, so I don't speak the language!"

Polly walked over to the sofa, turned
round and sat down! Have you ever seen
an elephant on a sofa? It's a very odd
sight! The sofa creaked and groaned
under Polly's weight.

I held my breath as I waited for the sofa to collapse. Alex rushed forward and jumped up beside Polly. He pushed against her huge grey back to try to get her to stand up.

"Polly, **move**!" Alex puffed. "If you b-break this sofa, I'm the one who'll g-get into trouble, not you." He looked at me. "Mike, don't just stand there. Come and help me."

I took a careful step onto the sofa.
I'd never been so close to an elephant in
my life. The fact that the elephant was
Alex's little sister didn't make her any
less scary.

The creaks and groans of the sofa
were really loud now. I reckoned it had
less than a minute of life left in it! At
any moment it was going to explode into
bits of wood and fabric all around us.

Alex and I pushed and heaved at Polly the elephant, but she refused to move.

"When I count to three, really **push**," Alex gasped, as we leaned against Polly. "OK. One! Two ..."

I was busy listening for Alex to say 'three', which was my big mistake. Just after he said 'two', Polly stood up and moved away while Alex and I were still leaning against her. We grabbed each other and tried to keep from falling, but ... CRASH!

We both fell off the sofa and onto the ground!

I bashed both my knees and got a mouth full of carpet fluff. It's hard to say who was more annoyed, me or Alex. Polly was really getting on my nerves now.

"Polly! Polly, put that down!" Alex rushed over to his sister, who had just picked up the fruit bowl off the dining table with her trunk.

Alex tried to get the bowl away from her, but Polly waved her trunk in the air above his head. I went over to help. We jumped up and down, up and down, but Polly's trunk was too high above us.

"Polly, don't drop that or you'll smash it!" Alex ordered. "Give it to me."

Polly did as Alex said. She gave it to him all right! She tipped all the fruit in the bowl on his head.

"Oww!" While Alex rubbed his sore head, Polly started to do something that made me back away from her.

"Alex ..." I began.

Polly was sucking up lots of peanuts from a dish on the table with her trunk. I had a horrible feeling ... and I was right!

Polly started to fire the peanuts at her brother and me. They smacked! They stung! They smarted! They **hurt**! I ran for cover, with Alex close behind me.

"I came round for some fun, not to be shot at with peanuts!" I grumbled.

Alex and I popped our heads up from behind the armchair. Polly started to trot towards us.

"Don't take another step," Alex commanded. But Polly just ignored him.

"Why don't you change us into something else?" I said to Alex. "Change us into mice. I read somewhere that elephants are scared of mice."

"I can't," Alex said. "I can only change three times a day and I've used them all up."

"But you were only a fly and a cat," I said. "That's two times."

"No, I was a fly **two** times," Alex said. "Remember?"

"So what are we going to do?" I
asked.

Polly the elephant was only a few
steps away from us now. We backed
away out of the room as she came closer
and closer.

"Polly, I'm warning you ..." But Alex didn't get any further.

By now we were out in the hall and Polly was still trotting towards us. She was half way through the door when it happened!

She got stuck! Well and truly stuck. She wiggled and jiggled but she couldn't move backwards, forwards or sideways.

"Serves you right, Polly," Alex said.

"Yeah! A double dose of serves you right with raspberry sauce on top!" I added.

Just at that moment, we heard a key in the front door.

"Mum! Mum's back!" Alex panicked.

But just as the door opened, Polly changed back into her 'normal' self. Alex scooped her up into his arms.

"Hi, Mum," he panted.

"Hello, Mummy!" Polly said. She stuck her thumb in her mouth and began to suck on it.

I couldn't believe it. She looked like a little angel in Alex's arms – as if she'd never do anything even a little bit bad.

"Hello, everyone!" Alex's mum smiled. "Alex, has Polly been good?"

"She hasn't caused any trouble at all, has she, Mike?" Alex said to me.

"No, Mrs Lessing," I said. "She's been really good." I crossed my fingers behind my back.

"Give her to me," Alex's mum said. "It's time for her nap."

"Pleased to." Alex handed his sister over. "Let's go over to your house, Mike." Then he said, under his breath, "Come on before Mum explodes when she sees all the fruit and peanuts on the carpet."

"My house will be boring after all this," I said as Alex's mum went upstairs with Polly.

"That's why I want to go over there," said Alex. "If your roof is hit by lightning and wild horses run into your kitchen, your house will still be quieter than this place!"

And you know something? He was right!

Our books are tested
for children and young people by
children and young people.

Thanks to everyone who consulted on
a manuscript for their time and effort in
helping us to make our books better
for our readers.